Magic Ballerina
Delphie and the Glass Slippers

Welcome to the world of Enchantia!

I have always loved to dance. The captivating
music and wonderful stories of ballet are so
inspiring. So come with me and let's follow
Delphie on her magical adventures in
Enchantia, where the stories of dance will
take you on a very special journey.

[signature] x

p.s. Turn to the back to learn a special
dance step from me...

Special thanks to
Linda Chapman and
Katie May

First published in Great Britain by HarperCollins *Children's Books* 2008
HarperCollins *Children's Books* is a division of HarperCollins *Publishers* Ltd,
77-85 Fulham Palace Road, Hammersmith, London W6 8JB

The HarperCollins *Children's Books* website address is
www.harpercollinschildrensbooks.co.uk

1

Text copyright © HarperCollins *Children's Books* 2008
Illustrations by Katie May
Illustrations copyright © HarperCollins *Children's Books* 2008

ISBN 978 0 00 785912 2

Printed and bound in England by
Clays Ltd, St Ives plc

Mixed Sources
Product group from well-managed
forests and other controlled sources
www.fsc.org Cert no. SW-COC-1806
© 1996 Forest Stewardship Council

FSC

FSC is a non-profit international organisation established to promote the
responsible management of the world's forests. Products carrying the FSC
label are independently certified to assure consumers that they come
from forests that are managed to meet the social, economic and
ecological needs of present and future generations.

Find out more about HarperCollins and the environment at
www.harpercollins.co.uk/green

Magic Ballerina

Delphie and the Glass Slippers

Darcey Bussell

HarperCollins *Children's Books*

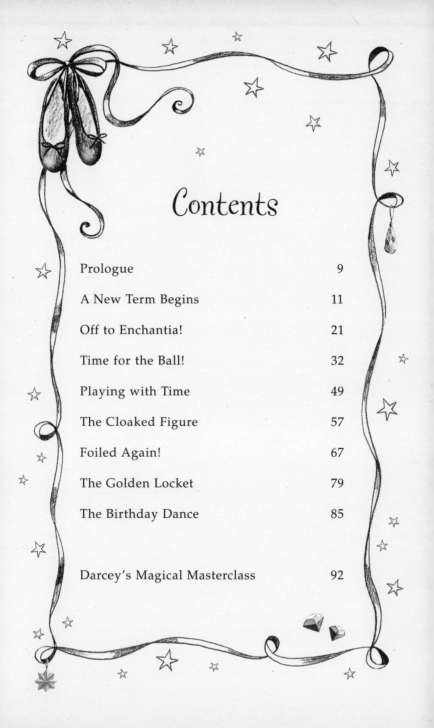

Contents

Prologue	9
A New Term Begins	11
Off to Enchantia!	21
Time for the Ball!	32
Playing with Time	49
The Cloaked Figure	57
Foiled Again!	67
The Golden Locket	79
The Birthday Dance	85
Darcey's Magical Masterclass	92

Prologue

*In the soft, pale light, the girl stood
with her head bent and her hands
held lightly in front of her.
There was a moment's silence and then
the first notes of the music began.
For as long as the girl could remember
music had seemed to tell her of
another world – a magical, exciting
world – that lay far, far away.
She always felt if she could just
close her eyes and lose herself,
then she would get there.
Maybe this time. As the music
swirled inside her, she swept
her arms above her head, rose on to
her toes and began to dance…*

A New Term Begins

Holding on to the *barre* with one hand,
Delphie Durand drew her toe up to her
knee and pointed her leg forward. *Head up,
back straight, shoulders down...* The thoughts
tumbled around in her head as she watched
herself in the mirror of the ballet studio.
Alongside her were nine other girls, all
gracefully performing the same exercise.

Barre work was quite repetitive and not as much fun as actually dancing in the centre of the room but Delphie was just glad to be doing ballet again. Madame Za-Za's School of Ballet had been closed for two weeks over the Christmas holidays and Delphie had really missed going to classes.

"Keep your knee turned out, Delphie. Graceful arms, please, Sukie." Madame Za-Za walked along the line gently correcting each girl. "Keep your body centred and straight, Poppy."

Delphie thought back to the last term. It had been such fun. The best bit had been dancing the main part in the school's Christmas show. *Actually, no,* she thought, correcting herself. The very best bit of last term had been finding out that the old red ballet shoes that Madame Za-Za had given her were magic!

The shoes could whisk Delphie away to Enchantia, a land where all the characters from different ballets lived. Delphie had been there many times now and she had always had an amazing adventure. *I wonder when I'll go there again*, she thought.

"Good," Madame Za-Za said finally when she reached the end of the line but as she turned away, Delphie saw her pass a hand over her forehead and sigh. Madame Za-Za looked very weary. "And to the

13

centre now, please, <u>girls</u>," she instructed.

The girls began to repeat the exercises in the centre of the room.

By the end of the class, Delphie's muscles were tingling from all the work. She felt tired but happy. Poppy and Lola, Delphie's two best friends, ran over to her. "Come on! Let's go and get <u>changed</u>!"

"In a minute," Delphie told them.

She went over to Madame Za-Za. The teacher smiled. "You danced very nicely today, Delphie," she said in her slight foreign accent.

"Thank you." A warm glow spread through Delphie at the praise. She hesitated. "<u>You</u>… <u>you look</u> tired, Madame Za-Za. Are you all right?"

Madame Za-Za sighed. "I am tired.

Sometimes I <u>wonder</u> if I am getting too old for all of this." She <u>swept</u> her hand around the dance studio.

Delphie stared at her. "You're not too old! Of course you're not!" Madame <u>Za-Za</u> had greying hair and there were a few wrinkles around the corners of her eyes but she could still dance really well and she was very elegant and beautiful. "You've got to keep teaching ballet!" <u>Delphie</u> said.

15

"Maybe it is just because it is my birthday next week that I am thinking like this," Madame Za-Za spoke gently. "I will be another year older – another year will have passed." She looked affectionately at Delphie. "Do not worry about me though, child."

Delphie joined Poppy and Lola feeling very worried.

"What was Madame Za-Za talking about?" Lola asked.

"I'll tell you when we get to Poppy's," said Delphie.

Back at Poppy's house the three girls hurried up to her bedroom. "So what's going on with Madame Za-Za?" Lola asked.

Delphie sat down cross-legged on
Poppy's large double bed and told her
friends what Madame Za-Za had said.

"But she can't give up teaching!" said
Poppy.

"No way. We won't let her!" said Lola.

"She didn't exactly say she *would* give up
teaching," said Delphie. "Only that she was
weary of it all. But maybe we can do
something that will make her remember
how good it is."

"Like what?" demanded Lola.

They all thought hard for a moment and then Delphie's eyes widened. "Perhaps we could try and cheer her up by learning a special dance? She said it was her birthday next week – we could perform it then. It would be our way of saying thank you for teaching us and telling her how much we love her classes."

"Oh yes!" breathed Poppy.

"That's a cool plan," said Lola. "We could try and work something out now?"

"Great!" said Delphie.

They began to talk about what music they could use and what dance they could do. It was hard to choose.

"I think *Swan Lake*!" said Lola. "We could all be swans."

"It's not very birthday-like though, is it?" said Poppy, just as her mum called them all for tea.

They sat down at the table. "How about we do a dance from *The Nutcracker*?" said Delphie. "We could use the music from The Land of Sweets."

They all nodded. "Let's try and make up a dance after tea," said Lola.

But when they tried, the music from The Land of Sweets seemed very fast and they kept losing track of where they were, and all ended up doing different things at different times.

"This isn't working," sighed Delphie. "If we show this to Madame Za-Za it'll be sure to make her want to give up teaching altogether!"

"Delphie! Lola! Your mums are here!" Poppy's mother called up the stairs.

"Let's all think about it tonight and phone each other tomorrow," Delphie suggested.

"Good plan." Poppy nodded as she waved Delphie and Lola off from the house.

Delphie ran down the steps and into her mother's waiting car. As she sat in the back seat on the way home, she stared out of the window. She so wanted them to perform something special for Madame Za-Za to make her smile. But what?

Off to Enchantia!

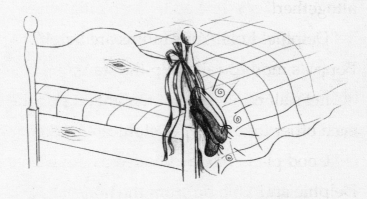

Delphie was still thinking about it when she went to bed that night and finally fell asleep. When she woke a little while later, the house was in darkness and quiet apart from a faint tinkling sound. Delphie's eyes flew to the end of her bed. Her red ballet shoes that were hanging there were sparkling and glowing. Delphie's heart leapt. Her friends in Enchantia needed her!

Jumping up, she started to put on the shoes, wondering what was happening. She was only ever whisked to Enchantia when there was a problem. *Where would she go?* Would it be to the theatre, which was the entrance to the magical world, or maybe she would go to Princess Aurelia's palace again? Excitement raced through Delphie as she crossed the ribbons around her ankles and tied them. She couldn't wait to find out!

As she finished tying the last ribbon she started to twirl round. The shoes spun her faster and faster until she was twirling in a haze of rainbow colours. She felt herself being lifted up and then coming down again. As her feet met the ground, the swirl of colours vanished and she opened her eyes.

She was standing in a dimly lit room, which had a wonky table, a little stool, a threadbare rug and a small hard bed. It didn't look like the beautiful royal palace and it certainly wasn't the theatre. So where was she?

Hearing the sound of crying, Delphie looked around. Behind her there was a fireplace with a few old embers glowing in the grate. A beautiful girl with long blonde hair was sitting beside it. She was wearing a ragged brown dress, an old shawl and she had a golden locket around her neck. She was so busy crying she hadn't seen Delphie.

"Um… hello," Delphie said.

The girl gasped. "Who are you?" She scrambled to her feet tucking the locket quickly inside her clothes.

"I'm Delphie."

The girl looked at Delphie's ballet shoes. "Of course. You're the girl with the red ballet shoes! Oh, have you come to help me?"

"I'll try," said Delphie. "What's your name and what's wrong?"

"I'm Cinderella, although everyone apart from my ugly sisters calls me Cinders. I'm supposed to be a princess by now and be married to my handsome prince but... oh!" Cinderella started to cry again. "Something's gone horribly wrong and it's all King Rat's fault!"

Delphie's heart sank. She'd met King Rat before and he was horrible. He lived in a smelly castle and he hated dancing. He was always trying to stop it and to cause problems for everyone else in Enchantia. "What's he done this time?" she said.

Cinderella pushed her long hair back from her face. "The whole thing started just after I became a princess. I was living in the palace and having such a lovely time. But then King Rat invited me and Prince Charming to a party at his castle. I didn't want to go because King Rat's so mean; I said no, and King Rat got really cross because he'd already told people that we would be there. He said we had to go and when I wouldn't he turned back time to before I became a princess to punish me. So now I'm back living here again and being bossed around by my ugly sisters."

"That's horrible," said Delphie. "But surely it'll be OK. If he's turned back time, all the things that happened will happen all over again.  You'll be invited to the ball, you'll see the fairy godmother and you'll meet Prince Charming. It'll be all right."

"It won't!" Cinders' voice rose to a wail. "Every night I see my fairy godmother and get to the ball all right, but as soon as I get there time jumps forward to midnight and then as the clock finishes chiming midnight,

27

time jumps back and I end up here in the afternoon before the ball again. King Rat has somehow cast a time-spell so it just keeps happening over and over again. I never meet the prince and I never get to leave my slipper and I always end up back in rags."

"Oh." Delphie didn't know what to say.

"Can you help me?" Cinderella begged.

"I'll try," Delphie promised.

"My fairy godmother should be here any moment," said Cinderella.

Delphie had just started to nod when there was a bright silver flash and Cinder's fairy godmother appeared. She was wearing a beautiful blue dress with a skirt that sparkled as if it was covered by stars.

"Oh, Cinders. I am sorry to see you here

again," she said sadly. "I wish I could do something and make the evening work out as it should."

"It's all right, Fairy Godmother," said Cinderella. "Delphie with the magic ballet shoes is here. She's going to try and help me."

A smile lit up the fairy godmother's face as she looked at Delphie. "Hello, Delphie. I have heard all about you from my friend the Sugar Plum Fairy." She danced over lightly on her toes and took Delphie's

29

hands. "I am so glad you are here. None of us can work out what type of spell King Rat has cast to change time like this so we don't know how to stop it. I really hope you can help us."

Delphie forced herself to smile but inside she was feeling worried. This seemed a really difficult problem to solve. If no one in Enchantia could work out how King Rat was doing the time-spell how would she be able to? *Still*, she reminded herself, *problems here always seem difficult but I've solved lots so far. Maybe I can help again.* She lifted

her chin. "I'll do my best," she said.

"Can Delphie come to the ball with me so she can see what happens?" asked Cinders eagerly.

"Of course she may," said her fairy godmother. "She can go as your seamstress. Have you got the pumpkin, the white mice and the frogs, Cinderella?"

Cinderella pulled out a pumpkin, a cage and a box from under her bed. "Of course I have!"

"Then let's take them outside and begin!" said the fairy godmother.

Time For the Ball!

Delphie and Cinderella took the pumpkin, mice and frogs outside, just as the sun was setting in the sky. The fairy godmother raised her wand and beautiful music flooded the air. She danced on to her pointes around Cinderella with tiny steps and then started turning quickly as she moved, arms held out to the sides so that it looked as if she was flying across the ground. Delphie watched as she stopped on her toes with one leg behind her, one arm stretched high and the other held gracefully in front as she pointed her wand at each of the objects in turn.

The pumpkin became a glittering carriage, the mice became four white horses, the frogs became a driver and a footman. Last but not least, the fairy godmother pointed her wand at Delphie and Cinderella. Delphie's nightdress turned into a long blue ballgown and Cinderella's ragged

outfit became a beautiful glittering white
dress with a long veil. She had a delicate
silver tiara in her hair, her gold locket
around her neck and dainty glass slippers
on her feet. But she didn't look delighted;
she just looked worried and sad.

The fairy godmother took their hands.
"You are now ready to go to the ball, girls.

Good luck!" She pirouetted around and
disappeared with another flash.

The footman held open the carriage door.
As Delphie waited for Cinders to get in, her
attention was caught by a clock tower at the
end of the street. It was
pearly white and the
gold numbers and
two gold hands
sparkled in the rays
of the setting sun.
"That's a beautiful
clock!" said
Delphie.

"That's the magic
clock of Enchantia,"
Cinderella told her. "It's
in charge of time here."

Something was glittering near the number twelve. Delphie frowned curiously. *What was it?* It didn't look part of the design of the clock face.

"Come on!" Cinders urged her.

Delphie stopped looking up and hastily got into the carriage. The horses tossed their heads and set off at a smart canter. It was an amazing feeling to be pulled through the cobbled streets of Enchantia, past little shops and tall houses crammed in side by side. There were people hurrying through the streets. None of them looked very happy. *No wonder*, thought Delphie. *It must be awful to repeat the same day over and over again.*

She glanced at Cinderella. "Will your…" Delphie hesitated, thinking it seemed a bit rude to say *ugly* sisters, "will your step-sisters be at the ball?"

"Oh yes," sighed Cinderella. "Augusta and June set off a while ago. I've been helping them get ready all afternoon. Unfortunately for you, you'll probably get to meet them!"

The coach stopped outside the Prince's palace. Delphie stared around in awe. Lights sparkled in the flowerbeds and great

pots around the palace overflowed with sweet-scented roses. Music flooded out from the open doors. Guests in beautiful outfits were getting out of carriages but, just like the people in the streets, they didn't look very happy. Cinderella led the way to the entrance, but just as they reached the palace doors a clock began to strike seven o'clock.

"Here we go again!" cried Cinders, grabbing Delphie's hand. Darkness fell and the whole world began to spin round as if it was a roundabout in a park. It got faster and faster and then suddenly stopped.

Delphie blinked. They were standing in exactly the same place outside the palace but now stars were twinkling in the night sky and the moon was shining.

"You see!" Cinderella said turning to Delphie in despair. "Time's jumped forward. It's midnight now. I haven't been inside and danced with the Prince so there's no point in me running away and leaving one of my glass slippers behind because he doesn't even know they belong to me!"

The clock inside the palace began to chime midnight.

"Everything's about to change again!" gasped Cinders. She squeezed Delphie's hands. "Hang on!"

As the clock reached the last stroke of midnight, the world went dark and began to spin round once more. But this time it felt like it was spinning backwards.

When it stopped, Delphie saw that the sun was high in the sky and Cinderella was wearing old brown rags again. The carriage had changed back to a pumpkin

41

and the horses to mice and the driver and footman to frogs.

"Come on!" sighed Cinderella. "It's back to the afternoon before the ball now. Let's go home." She sighed. "I'm afraid it's quite a long walk."

As they trudged back to Cinderella's house, Delphie thought hard. She wished there was something she could do to help. But what *could* she do? She really had no idea.

As they reached Cinderella's street, Delphie looked at the clock tower. Again, she caught sight of something on the clock face near the number twelve, glinting in the rays of the sun. *Just what is it?* she wondered.

Delphie touched Cinders' arm. "Cinders, can you see that thing sparkling on the clock?"

"There isn't anything that sparkles on…" Cinders broke off. "Oh yes! I see what you mean. There *is* something there."

"Maybe whatever is glinting has something to do with why the time keeps changing," said Delphie thoughtfully. "We should investigate."

"But how?" asked Cinderella. "The clock tower's really high."

Delphie had an idea. "I know. Why don't we ask the Sugar Plum Fairy? She could fly up there!"

"Sugar? Oh yes," breathed Cinders. "Do you know her? I'd love to meet her!"

"Yes, I know her," said Delphie. "We've had many an adventure together."

"But how do we get her here?" asked Cinders.

Delphie thought hard. She knew it was possible to summon people in Enchantia by doing the dance from the ballet they came from. She raised her arms and tried to remember a little bit of the Sugar Plum Fairy's dance. It was hard because Sugar often danced on pointes and Delphie

44

couldn't do that yet but she danced as high on her toes as she could. She danced in a circle, turning rapidly and keeping her movements as light and graceful as she could. Then she stopped in an arabesque with one leg lifted off the ground behind her, just as she had once seen Sugar do.

Suddenly there was a lilac flash and the Sugar Plum Fairy appeared.

"Sugar!" Delphie cried, rushing forwards to meet her friend.

"Hello, Delphie," Sugar said, hugging her. "It's lovely to see you again."

"This is Cinderella," Delphie said.

The Sugar Plum Fairy took Cinders' hands. "Isn't this time-spell horrible? I've been trying to work out what we can do

about it for days. But it's worse for you than the rest of us – never getting to meet your handsome prince and to have to keep being a servant instead of a princess."

"It is," said Cinders sadly.

"So why did you call me?" Sugar asked Delphie. "Do you think you can help us do something about it?"

"I don't know," said Delphie thoughtfully. "But there seems to be something strange on the clock face and we don't know what it is or if it's important." Delphie pointed. "Can you see it glittering near the twelve?"

"Oh yes," Sugar said. "There isn't normally anything there."

"Maybe that's what causing the problems with time." Delphie gave Sugar a hopeful look. "Would you be able to fly up there and take a look?"

"Of course!"

Delphie watched eagerly as Sugar pirouetted round and rose into the air, her wings fluttering.

What was she going to find?

Playing with Time

As Sugar hovered in front of the clock, Delphie and Cinderella saw her peer closer, run her wand over the face and then reach forwards and pull something out.

What was it? Delphie could barely contain her excitement.

The Sugar Plum Fairy flew down. "Look!" she exclaimed, waving a glass slipper in the air. "This was jammed into the clock face!"

"A glass slipper!" exclaimed Cinders as Sugar landed.

The slipper was large with a high heel, a pointed toe that curled upwards and covered in gaudy blue, green and red jewels.

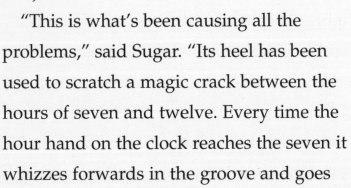

"This is what's been causing all the problems," said Sugar. "Its heel has been used to scratch a magic crack between the hours of seven and twelve. Every time the hour hand on the clock reaches the seven it whizzes forwards in the groove and goes

straight to midnight. When the hour hand gets to midnight it bumps into the glass slipper and bounces all the way back to the afternoon taking everyone back in time!"

"So that's how King Rat has been doing his time-spell," Delphie said to Cinderella.

"Yes! I bet it's one of his ball slippers!" said Cinders, looking at the ugly shoe. "He wouldn't mind giving it up because he hates dancing anyway."

"So now that we've got it out of the clock does that mean that everything will be all right?" Delphie asked eagerly. "Will time work normally for Cinderella again?"

"Yes!" said Sugar. "I mended the crack with my wand while I was up there and now the clock is working perfectly again."

Delphie and Cinders hugged each other.

"Oh, Delphie, maybe tonight I'll meet my prince properly!" said Cinders.

Just then the window of the house flew open and an older girl with a long nose, pointed chin and three big warts looked out. "Cinders, you ugly little woodlouse!" she bellowed. "What are you doing lazing around out there? I've been calling and calling for you. Hurry in here this minute and get me ready for the ball!"

"Yes, Augusta," Cinders said quickly.

"So there you are, you little worm!" the window on the other side of the house flew open and June looked out. "I've been shouting your name for an hour. I need you to file my toe-nails."

"And I need you to trim the hairs on my warts and shampoo my hair," said Augusta.

"She's to help me first!" said June.

"No, me!"

"Me!"

"ME!"

Cinders sighed as her sisters shrieked above her head. "I'd better go," she said apologetically to Delphie and Sugar. "Hopefully this is the last time I have to get them ready for the ball."

"Would you like me to help you?" Delphie offered.

"I couldn't ask that," replied Cinders in a
low voice. "You can see what they're like.
They're horrible! Besides, they would
wonder where you had come from."

At that moment, both sisters looked at
her and shrieked. "Cinders, get in here NOW!"

"It's OK," Delphie said bravely. "I don't
mind helping." She took Cinders' hand.
"And I'm sure we can think of something
as to who I am. Come on, I'll help you get
them ready."

"And I'll go and tell your fairy godmother
what's been happening," said Sugar,
dancing away. "See you both at the ball."

The two ugly sisters were more than happy
to boss Delphie around too. Delphie had

never worked so hard in her life! They
made her wash their hair and dry it and
put it in great big purple rollers. She had to
massage them with cream, file away the

hard skin on their feet
and pluck hairs from
their ears with tweezers,
and all the time they
shouted and nagged
her.

"You're pulling
my hair!"

"Ow! That hurts!"

"Can't you work
any faster? I'm never
going to be ready in
time!"

By the time six o'clock came and the ugly sisters were in their bright ballgowns, Delphie was exhausted. She collapsed with Cinders on the hard floor of her tiny room.

"Now we just have to wait for the Fairy Godmother," said Cinderella. "Thank you for helping, Delphie. You're a real friend."

The fairy godmother was full of excitement when she arrived. "Oh, I hope tonight you meet your prince, my dear," she said to Cinderella as she magicked her rags away and turned Delphie's nightdress into a ballgown again. "Have a good time, both of you!"

Delphie grinned at Cinderella. "I hope we will!"

The Cloaked Figure

Delphie and Cinderella arrived at the ball on the stroke of seven. As the clock began to chime, Delphie held her breath and Cinders gripped her arm. But nothing happened! The clock reached the seventh note and everything stayed exactly as it was. No darkness fell; there was no feeling of rushing.

"We've really done it!" gasped Cinders. "We've broken King Rat's time-spell!"

Delphie grinned in delight and felt relief flood through her.

"Come on!" Cinders said, grabbing her hand. "Let's go and enjoy the ball!"

Inside the palace, there was a massive ballroom with a domed roof. A band was playing. People were dancing and servants were hurrying around, offering people drinks. Delphie took a glass of fruit punch. It tasted delicious like strawberries and peaches mixed up together with lots of ice. She could see Augusta and June dancing with two young men who both looked like they would rather be somewhere else. Their toes were being trodden on and they were being bossed around.

"No, not like that! Hold me tighter!"
Augusta was complaining.

"You're not spinning me round
properly," June moaned to her partner.
"And you haven't once told me how
beautiful I am!"

In another room there were huge tables
with white tablecloths; throughout the
other rooms there were comfy chairs and
sofas to sit on and outside in the garden
there were jugglers, fire-eaters and men
walking on stilts.

"Oh, I love this music!" said Cinderella
as the band started to play a march. She
and Delphie went through to the ballroom.
A procession of palace servants was
marching with huge trays of food. It was all
so beautiful. The servants laid the food

down carefully on the tables before dancing together, one way and then the other. Then they all marched on the spot, their arms coming above their heads as they made a circle. Delphie watched, enchanted; she could feel herself aching to join in.

An idea hit her. Maybe she, Poppy and Lola could do a march like that for Madame Za-Za!

But then she was distracted by a gasp from Cinderella. She looked around. The Prince, wearing a white and gold jacket, was standing at Cinderella's side. "You are finally here," he said softly. "Will you dance?"

Cinderella nodded wordlessly and taking her hand, he led her on to the centre of the floor as the march finished and the band struck up a waltz.

Delphie sipped her punch and watched as the Prince put his arm round Cinderella's waist and they began to dance. She had never seen two people waltz so lightly. The Prince spun Cinderella around the room as if she was as light as thistledown. Their eyes never left each other's faces.

Delphie smiled in delight.

"It's all working out perfectly," a voice said beside her. She looked round and saw Sugar standing beside her.

"It is," Delphie said happily.

The Prince and Cinderella danced all night and then at midnight, just as happened in the fairytale, Cinderella broke away from him and ran out of the palace. As she ran one of her glass slippers came off.

Sugar and Delphie were watching from the garden. "I think your job is done, Delphie," said Sugar softly. "Everything is happening just as it should."

Delphie looked down at her ballet shoes, expecting them to sparkle as they usually did when things had all worked out in Enchantia. But they didn't. "The shoes aren't taking me home," she said.

"Maybe the magic is going to let you stay so that you can see the Prince find Cinderella tomorrow," Sugar said. "In which case, why don't I take us to my

home so we can get some rest? We can
come back to Cinderella's house tomorrow
morning to watch her trying on the glass
slipper and see the Prince asking her to
marry him."

"Oh yes!" Delphie breathed. She'd love
to see that.

Sugar waved her wand. Lilac sparkles
flew out and swirled round them. They
started to spin round. As they did, Delphie
glanced back at where the glass slipper was
lying. Would she see the Prince running out
to pick it up?

To her surprise she saw someone, but it
wasn't the Prince. It was a figure covered in
a hooded cloak. They hurried out from
behind a rose bush and bent over the
slipper but before Delphie could see what

they did, she was whisked away in a
sparkling cloud.

As she spun through the air to Sugar's
house she felt a flicker of unease. Who was
that in the cloak? Why had they been
looking at the slipper?

It's probably just one of the servants, she
thought. Maybe it was just someone who
wasn't mentioned in the fairytale. *Everything's
going to be all right*, she told herself, pushing
the strange sighting from her mind. *It has
to be!*

Foiled Again!

Delphie stayed the night in a beautiful rose-pink bedroom at Sugar's house. She and the fairy had breakfast and then Sugar whisked them both back to Cinderella's street.

"The Prince's manservant should be there by now with the glass slipper," Sugar said. "He'll have been going around all the houses this morning seeing who the glass slipper fits."

They landed opposite Cinderella's house. The street was crowded with lots of the townspeople watching what was going on and Cinderella's front door was open. The manservant was outside with a glass slipper on a purple cushion. Augusta, June and Cinderella were standing in the street.

"It fits me best!" Augusta was saying, glaring at June.

"No, it fits me!" snapped June, grabbing the shoe. "*I'm* going to marry the Prince!"

"No, *I* am!" said Augusta, trying to pull the shoe off her.

"Ladies, ladies!" said the manservant hastily, trying to take hold of the slipper.

"Shove off!" Augusta said, pushing him hard and sending him sprawling into the gutter.

"I don't understand! It should fit me!" said Cinderella, bursting into tears.

"Something must have gone wrong!" exclaimed Sugar. "That's not even Cinderella's slipper. Look! It's like the one in the clock!"

She was right. The slipper the ugly sisters were playing tug of war with was big and covered with bright jewels.

"What's happened?" said Delphie.

Suddenly she heard the sound of chortling laughter. It was coming from a nearby alleyway.

Delphie went over and looked down it. What she saw made her gasp. "Sugar!" she hissed, beckoning Sugar over. "King Rat's here with some of his mouse guards!"

They peered cautiously round the corner. King Rat had his back to them. He was wearing a dark cloak and boots and had a golden crown on his head. Five of his mouse guards were gathered round him. They were all bigger than Delphie and had sharp swords slung into their belts. Their teeth were pointed and their eyes gleamed.

"Oh, I am so clever!" King Rat preened the black greasy fur on top of his head. "That interfering girl and annoying fairy thought they had foiled my plan but now the Prince will have to marry one of the ugly sisters and Cinderella will never be happy again!"

"How did you do it, sire?" asked one of the mice.

"It's easy when you have brains!" boasted King Rat. "I simply waited for Cinderella to run out and leave her glass slipper behind. Before the Prince came out, I swapped it for one of my own. Then I smashed Cinderella's slipper so it can never be found and so she won't get to marry her Prince!"

"Genius, sire!" said one of the mice.

"It is rather, even if I say so myself," said King Rat. He glared round at his other guards. "You can all say it too."

"You're a genius, sire," the mice said quickly. "A genius!"

King Rat sniggered. "That will teach Cinderella to turn down invitations to my castle!"

Delphie pulled Sugar back. "What are we going to do?" She couldn't believe everything had gone so wrong. King Rat was right. Now Cinderella wouldn't get to marry the Prince. She felt awful. "Oh if only we could change the slipper for the one that fits Cinderella's foot, but it's been smashed."

Sugar stared at her. "Perhaps there's a way!" she exclaimed. "You see I can use my magic to transform things. All we'd need to do is get near enough to King Rat's slipper so that I could touch it with my wand and transform it into Cinderella's! Oh, Delphie, it's a great idea!"

Sugar began to dance. Music echoed faintly through the air but everyone else was too caught up in the argument to notice it. Everyone apart from Cinderella.

She looked up and seeing Sugar dancing towards her, her face lit up with hope.

Sugar placed a finger to her lips and danced past the manservant and up to the ugly sisters almost before anyone knew what was happening.

74

But King Rat realised! "No!" he roared, running out of the alleyway. "Stop that fairy!"

Delphie gasped as lots of things suddenly seemed to happen at once.

The ugly sisters and manservant turned to look at King Rat and the guards as they burst out of the alleyway. Seeing them heading for Sugar, Delphie jumped in front of the first one and stuck her foot out. He tripped over and fell to the ground with a loud yell. The other guards tumbled over him, ending up in a large sprawling heap.

"You idiots!" yelled King Rat.

While everyone was staring at King Rat and the mice in astonishment, Sugar touched the shoe with her wand. With a faint flash of lilac light it transformed into Cinderella's glass slipper. There was a clatter of hooves and the Prince came cantering down the street on a white stallion. He stopped outside Cinderella's house just at the right moment.

"I hear the person has been found whose foot fits the slipper!" he exclaimed.

"Not just person," said the manservant, looking flustered. "But persons, your Highness. There are actually two of them. Well, there were," he said, doing a double take as he looked down at the slipper in his hand.

"It fits me!" said Augusta, snatching the slipper off the manservant and trying to force her foot inside. But the  slipper was much too small now.

"I told you it fits me better!" said June, grabbing the slipper from Augusta and trying to push her toes inside.

"It doesn't fit either of them!" shouted Delphie, racing forwards, unable to keep quiet any longer. "It fits Cinderella!"

There was a moment's silence and then Cinderella stepped forwards.

The Prince smiled at her. "I think it will fit you."

Cinderella put the slipper on. It fitted her perfectly. "Yes," she said, looking up at him and holding out her foot. "It does."

The Prince leapt down from his horse and knelt on the cobbles.

"Will you marry me?"

"Oh yes!" Cinderella breathed. "I will!"

The Golden Locket

Delphie and Sugar hugged as the Prince swept Cinderella into an embrace.

"No!" bellowed King Rat, stamping his feet in fury.

Augusta marched over to him. "If I can't have the Prince, *you'll* do."

"I saw him first," said June, going up to the other side and grabbing his arm.

She batted her eyelashes at him. "Hello, Handsome!"

"Help!" King Rat exclaimed, shaking himself free. "I'm off!" He turned and ran up the street with the ugly sisters chasing after him.

"Come back!" they screeched.

The mice looked at each other, shrugged and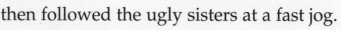

then followed the ugly sisters at a fast jog.

Delphie and Sugar giggled.

"Oh, Delphie, it really has worked out perfectly after all!" said Sugar as the Prince clicked his fingers and music flooded magically through the air. It was the waltz

from the night before. The Prince spun Cinderella round, their feet flying over the rough cobbles. As Cinderella swept past Delphie, she pulled momentarily out of the Prince's arms.

"Thank you, Delphie!" she cried, her blue eyes shining with joy. "Thank you so much!"

"That's OK," said Delphie happily. "I'm just glad it's all sorted."

Cinderella took out her golden locket. "Please will you take this 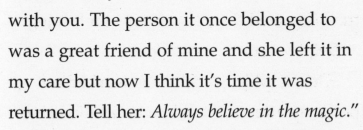 with you. The person it once belonged to was a great friend of mine and she left it in my care but now I think it's time it was returned. Tell her: *Always believe in the magic*."

"But who does it belong to?" Delphie asked.

Before Cinderella could reply, the Prince had whisked her away.

As all of the townspeople joined in with the waltz, Delphie didn't have time to think about what Cinderella had said. She slipped the locket round her neck as Sugar grabbed her hands. Delphie had never really waltzed before but she let her feet in the magic shoes guide her. She and Sugar twirled lightly up and down the street. It felt like flying!

Delphie's feet began to tingle. Looking down she saw that the red shoes were glowing. "I'm about to go home, Sugar!" she gasped.

"See you soon!" cried Sugar.

"Bye!" called Delphie as, in a haze of swirling light, she was whisked away...

She landed with a slight bump in her bedroom. It was dark and quiet after the music and light of Enchantia. Her hand reached round her neck. Yes, she still had the locket. She carefully took it off and opened it. Inside there were two pictures. One of Cinderella smiling and another of a girl with big brown eyes and browny-red hair. She looked very familiar. *Just like*

Madame Za-Za must have looked when she was younger.

Delphie's hand flew to her mouth. Her ballet teacher had hinted that she had been to Enchantia too. Maybe this *was* a picture of her! Maybe she had once been friends with Cinderella?

Delphie closed the locket slowly. She realised she'd just found the perfect present for Madame Za-Za's birthday.

The Birthday Dance

On the following Saturday afternoon, Delphie, Poppy and Lola got to the ballet school early. They had told Madame Za-Za they had a surprise for her.

"Happy birthday, Madame Za-Za," they all called, running in with the chocolate cake they had made that morning. "We've got you a cake and made up a dance for you for your birthday!"

"Really?" Madame Za-Za said. "That is lovely of you, girls. The cake looks delicious!"

They quickly got changed and then Delphie put the CD of music from *Cinderella* into the machine. As she ran to her starting position she looked at Madame Za-Za sitting in her chair. Her face looked strained.

I hope this works, Delphie thought anxiously as she took her place behind Poppy and Lola.

The music from the ballet of *Cinderella* flooded out. Delphie saw Madame Za-Za blink and straighten up slightly but then the march began and all of Delphie's attention was focused on dancing. She, Poppy and Lola had been practising all week.

They stepped forwards, with Poppy and Lola pretending they were carrying something and Delphie in between them carrying the locket, wrapped up in pink tissue paper.

They stopped in a line behind each other and then Poppy and Lola danced to the left and Delphie danced to the right, stepping

lightly, spinning round and stopping up on their toes with their arms above their heads. Then they stepped back again and spun round as they got back into their line, ending with their knees bent. Marching around the room, their heads were held high, and they had smiles on their faces. They turned together, perfectly in time.

One turn, two turns, three turns. Delphie passed Madame Za-Za and saw a smile on her teacher's face. Her head was nodding in time with the music.

Finally the girls stopped in front of her.

"Beautiful! Just beautiful, girls!" Madame Za-Za exclaimed.

"If it was, it's because you've taught us so well." Delphie handed her the present. "Happy birthday, Madame Za-Za."

"A present?" said Madame Za-Za, as she unwrapped it. "But you shouldn't have got me a…" Her voice faltered as she pulled back the tissue and saw the locket. "Oh," she whispered.

"There's a message with it," Delphie said softly. She saw Poppy and Lola glance at each other. They had asked her where the

locket had come from but she had just
made up a story that she had found it in a
junk shop and pretended she herself was
going to make up a message. *"Always
believe in the magic."*

Madame Za-Za looked at her and, for a
moment a look of understanding passed
between them.

"Then that is what I shall do," Madame
Za-Za said softly. A smile spread across her
face. "Maybe I'm *not* too old for this life of
teaching after all."

"Of course you're not!" said Lola.

"This music is too hard to resist. May I dance with you, girls?"

"Yes!" they all cried.

Madame Za-Za stood up, danced forwards and spun into a pirouette followed by a leap in the air. Forgetting the moves they had learned, the girls grinned happily and with whatever steps came into their heads, started dancing around the room with their ballet teacher.

Darcey's Magical Masterclass

The Cinderella Sweep

Cinderella might not enjoy sweeping the floor for her horrible sisters, but she loves this graceful leg sweep. Ballerinas call these movements Battement tendu...

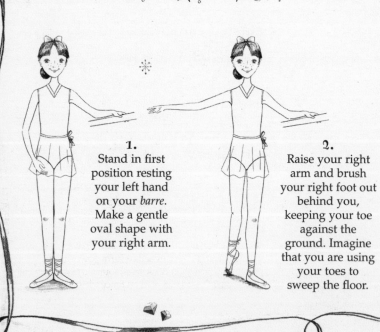

1.
Stand in first position resting your left hand on your *barre*. Make a gentle oval shape with your right arm.

2.
Raise your right arm and brush your right foot out behind you, keeping your toe against the ground. Imagine that you are using your toes to sweep the floor.

3.
Sweep your foot
back to the centre
and then brush it out
to the side.

4.
Now slide your foot
back to the centre
again. Try switching
sides to practise
using your left leg.

(P.S. If you don't have
an actual *barre* you
could rest your hand on
a wall or fence instead.)

Magic Ballerina™

Delphie and the Fairy Godmother

Princess Aurelia has fallen under a wicked
spell and just won't wake up! Can Delphie and
Lila, the princesses's fairy godmother, find the
prince who can break the spell or will everyone
in Enchantia remain asleep forever?

**Read on for a sneak preview
of book five...**

Delphie looked round and saw a beautiful ballerina appear in a shimmering haze. Dressed in a lilac tutu with a sparkling bodice, her brown hair was caught up in a diamond tiara. The ballerina's arms were held high above her head and she was carrying a wand in her right hand.

"Delphie!" the fairy cried. "I'm so glad you've come!"

"Hi. Who are you?" Delphie asked.

"I'm The Lilac Fairy from *Sleeping Beauty*. Lila for short, and one of Princess Aurelia's fairy godmothers " the fairy answered. "Oh, Delphie, we're in real trouble," she cried. "The Royal Palace has been covered with thorns and is now hidden behind these brambles. Everyone in the palace is asleep including Aurelia. She'll only wake up when a prince – her one true love – kisses her…" Lila bit her lip. "The trouble is I've been trying to find him but he seems to have disappeared!"

"Disappeared?" Delphie echoed.

° ⊙ ˙* ☆ ⊙ ˙* ☆ ⊙ ˙* ☆ ⊙ ˙* °

Darcey Bussell

Buy more great Magic Ballerina books direct from HarperCollins
at 10% off recommended retail price.
FREE postage and packing in the UK.

Delphie and the Magic Ballet Shoes	ISBN 978 0 00 728607 2
Delphie and the Magic Spell	ISBN 978 0 00 728608 9
Delphie and the Masked Ball	ISBN 978 0 00 728610 2
Delphie and the Glass Slippers	ISBN 978 0 00 728617 1
Delphie and the Fairy Godmother	ISBN 978 0 00 728611 9
Delphie and the Birthday Show	ISBN 978 0 00 728612 6

All priced at £3.99

To purchase by Visa/Mastercard/Switch simply call
08707871724 or fax on **08707871725**

To pay by cheque, send a copy of this form with a cheque made payable to
'HarperCollins Publishers' to: Mail Order Dept. (Ref: BOB4),
HarperCollins Publishers, Westerhill Road, Bishopbriggs, G64 2QT,
making sure to include your full name, postal address and phone number.